THE ADVENTURES OF Seymour & Hau
Morocco

Melanie Morse & Thomas McDade

Illustrated by: John Soleas & Jon Westwood

A **HONEY+PUNCH** BOOK

Honey + Punch LLC - info@honeyandpunch.com

ISBN 978-0-692-29834-3

Published by: Honey + Punch LLC

First Edition

The Adventures of Seymour & Hau: Morocco © 2014

For Jacob, Elliot & Charlie, with love -MM

For Molly, Allison & Nathan -TM

Thank you!

We are so incredibly thankful to our friends and family for endless love, support, advice and all the good things you can think of. Special thanks to; Patty (aka Melanie's Mom), Tom & Carole McDade (Tom's folks), Brain Donovan, Tempany Deckart, Barbara Canazzi, and Brendan Conners. Extra special thanks to the magnificent Mike Gelen, for helping bring our buddies Seymour and Hau to life for the first time. Angela Hastings, Rob Graham, and Mike Cammarata for their editing skeels (we spelled that wrong on purpose). Miss Caitlin at Tapestry Charter School for letting us share our book. And finally, to a few really great guys, Jacob, Elliot and Charlie Morse, for reading, listening, helping, and being so excited. We love you people.

We also want to pre-thank our agent and publisher. You are the best and we can't wait to meet you!

Morocco

TABLE OF CONTENTS

INTRODUCTION

Me

Hi, I'm Seymour and I'm 11. I live with my mom and two younger brothers. I love playing street hockey, soccer, and bass guitar. I used to be a normal kid until Hau showed up. I'm actually still normal, if you call normal going on wild adventures and getting my life threatened to help kids from all over the world.

Besides that, everything is the same, except that I'm hanging with a mega-galactic alien and my closet smells gross.

Hau

loodbraeee lkjie DiF m nz eee untyde ooe lnrz 4Tleark mho ... sobveh eee

Translation

My name is Hau. Take me to your leader earthling. LOL! My people think I needed to learn some "life lessons" so they sent me to earth. Seymour is helping me to get back home. So far the life lessons

I learned are: I love Earth people, Earth food and TV, especially The Voice, and Ellen Degeneres and Dr. Phil, but don't tell anyone about that last one. I live in Seymour's closet and everyone here thinks I smell gross.

My Mom

My mom's name is Helen and she is the coolest mom on the planet. She doesn't yell...too much. I can't tell her about Hau, but she is getting suspicious. I heard her talking to my grandma on the phone and she said, "That boy is acting so strange lately. He's always telling stories about different countries. It's almost as if he travels in his sleep." Can you believe that? I'd better be more careful. She also said, "... and his closet smells awful, I can't figure out what it might be." Let's hope she doesn't!

How I Met Hau

I swear, I thought this was SPAM until Hau stumbled out of my closet.

To: Seymour
From: Morgeeta Dispatcher
Subject: Hau's Arrival

Seymour,
You have been chosen to help Hau regain his place on our planet. He has been sent to Earth to earn his way back. You will be sent on great adventures, face danger and help kids around the world. We cannot guarantee your safety but you will be rewarded when your mission in complete. You will be tested and return tired but no time will pass at home. We are watching, and Hau's return will depend on your success.

Best of luck,

Oruk
Dispatch Director
Morgeeta, Milky Way Galaxy

The Tellus

Hau has got this AWESOME little machine that he keeps in his pouch. It's called a TELLUS, and it "tells us" where we need to go and who we need to help. Get it? Tell Us. I'm dead serious that's what it's called. It kind of looks like a cell phone with flashing lights all over it. It's connected to Hau's planet somehow. They know EVERTHING that's happening on Earth. They are always watching us. Bizarre. There's a map on it too, and a little black dot that blinks in the spot where we have to go. It also helps us with *The Leap*. There's a bunch of other buttons on it too, but we haven't figure out what they do yet.

The Pouch

OK, so Hau has this pouch. It's kind of like a kangaroo pouch but he can pull just about anything out of it - except maybe not a baby kangaroo. They all have pouches on his planet. I don't know EXACTLY what's in there.

It's really random. I don't think even Hau knows, but I have seen him pull everything from a wheelbarrow to a 'Kiss Me I'm Irish' t-shirt out of that thing. Now, if he could only pull out some soap...

The Leap Closet

It's really my bedroom closet. It looks like a normal bedroom closet; games on the shelf, clothes on the floor. The usual. However, when *The Leap* happens, the closet is totally NOT NORMAL. Once we shut the door, Hau pushes a button on the Tellus and everything turns the color of tie-dye. Then, it feels like you're on a crazy roller coaster ride and you land in a far away place. It is SO FUN! The Leap Closet is also Hau's bedroom...which is why it reeks.

Marrakech, Morocco

A little more info about Morocco & Marrakech:

This is what the Moroccan flag looks like.

This is what Arabic writing looks like.

وَعَلَيْكُمُ السَّلاَم

←

A cool thing about Arabic is that you read from right to left.

This says - As-salamu alaykum, which means: "peace be upon you", a common greeting in Morocco.

Full name of Morocco: The Kingdom of Morocco

Location: Continent of Africa

The official language: Arabic, but a lot of languages are spoken including: Berber, French & Spanish

The money is called: Dirhams

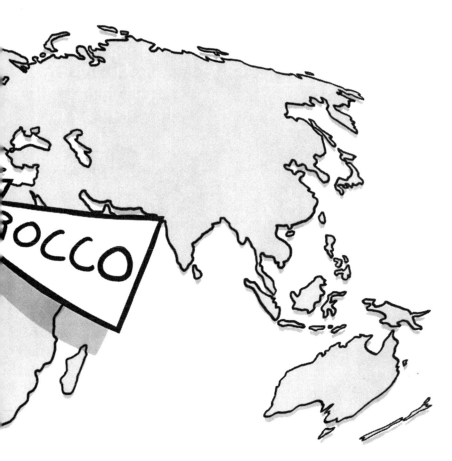

Here are some other Arabic words:

What is your name? --- ma ismok?

Nice to meet you --- tasharrafna

Goodbye --- ma'assalama

Hello --- marhaba

Good Morning --- sabah al-hayri

How are you? --- kayfa haluk?

Stuff to Know About Camels

Dromedary Camels
are in Morocco

1 Hump

Bactrian Camels are
not in Morocco

2 Humps

There are 2 kinds of camels in the world, dromedary camels and bactrian camels. Dromedary camels have 1 hump and bactrian camels have 2 humps. You will only find dromedary camels in Morocco.

The dromedary camel, also known as the Arabian camel, exists today only as a domesticated animal. About 90 percent of the world's camels are dromedaries.

Domesticated = tame and kept as a pet or on a farm.

Some Camel Facts

- Camels have a reputation for spitting but they don't actually spit, it would be a waste of water. They are actually throwing up on you. GROSS!!

- A camel's poop is so dry you can set it on fire. Don't try that at home.

- Baby camels are born without a hump. They won't get one until they start eating solid food.

- Camels can close their nostrils to keep sand out of their noses. Kind of like nose doors.

- Camels can go a week or more without water, and they can last for way longer without food.

1 BIZARRE

"SEYMOUR!!!" my mom yelled.

I pretended not to hear her because I was just about to get to the next level of Astroplanet on my video game, and I knew it was way past my bedtime.

"SEYMOUR JOSEPH!!! GET IN HERE!"

Yep, I was in trouble. When your mom uses your middle name attached to your first name, you just know. For like, a second, I thought maybe she found Hau, so, I closed my video game and shuffled off toward her voice.

My mom was in the laundry room standing on top of the dryer. I had never seen her do this before. It was bizarre. She was just staring at me. Her eyes were as big as flying saucers.

1

She slowly pointed to my favorite jeans in a lump on the floor.

"Wh-Wh-What is in that pocket?" Her voice still sounded really freaked out.

Now, I was getting freaked out! I picked up my jeans, reached into the pocket and pulled out a dead three-inch cockroach.

"Oh, yeah!" I thought to myself. I remembered immediately. I found it when Hau and I were in Australia last week.

I was going to keep him in a box and feed him until he was the biggest cockroach in the world. I was going to be in the *Guinness Book of World Records*. I guess I'd forgotten about him because the poor guy was all dried up.

AUSTRALIA

I once read that cockroaches could live for ten days without a head, but I guess not that long in the pocket of your jeans, even with a head.

My mom wasn't interested in explanations. Mom doesn't like bugs. At all. She made me check all the other pockets in all my jeans and sent me to bed. Sheesh! She didn't seem to mind so much when my backpack was full of orangutan hair from Indonesia. She just looked at me like I was bizarre.

So there I was, on my bed. Again. Listening to Hau snore in my closet. Again. That's when it happened. Again!

2 LEAPING AND LANDING

BBUUUZZZZAAAAPPPPT! BBUUUZZZZAAAAPPPPT! BBUUUZZZZAAAAPPPPT!

It was the TELLUS. That is when the fun begins!

When the TELLUS buzzes, the same thing happens every time, and it cracks me up! It happens just like this:

1. I watch Hau's eyes pop open really big (flying saucers).
2. He bangs his head on the clothes rack and knocks down all the hangers.
3. He searches through his pouch and tosses out random things that are in his way. Usually old food.
4. He says, "HA AH." (Did I mention he says things backwards sometimes?).
5. He finds the TELLUS and shouts out where we are going.

I love making lists, it's my thing

All of that only takes about seventeen seconds, but it is SO FUNNY to watch! You have GOT to see it sometime.

This time, he shouted, "To Marrakech, Morocco, Away, and Up, Up!" Obviously, he has read a few of my comic books, and he LOVES Superman.

I have hardly ever heard of anyplace we have to go, and this time was no different.

"Where the heck is Marrakech, Morocco? Pass me the TELLUS," I said. I took one look and knew right away. The little black dot was blinking right at the top of Africa.

If there is anything I remember from school it's the continents. My first grade teacher, Mrs. Houston, made us learn this song OVER AND OVER about the continents. She would point to them and we had to sing, everyday, like 11 times.

Incidentally... (I love the word incidentally.
It means I'm going to tell you something
extra just because I feel like it.)

Incidentally, Mrs. Houston lives right on my
block! I thought teachers were supposed
to live on school grounds. How would you
like it if you were just walking to the
corner store to buy a root beer and you
felt like someone was going to step outside and ask you 'what is eight times
four'? It's very freaky, and I hate the
eights.

So, we were going to Africa. Africa is SO
AWESOME! They have pyramids there, in Egpyt,
and nothing is awesomer than mummies. But, we
were not going to the Egypt part of Africa. We were
going to Morocco, which is WAY WEST of Egypt.

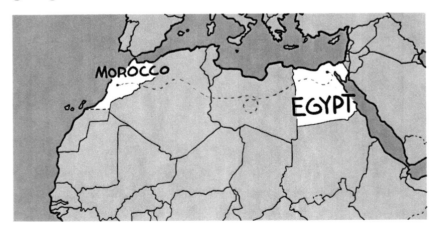

On the map, Marrakech, Morocco looked kind of
'desertish'. I grabbed my backpack, made sure I had

6

a full water bottle, and I was ready to go!

It was time for *The Leap*.

The Leap is when Hau zaps us to the country we need to go to. I call it *The Leap* because we appear in a new country in the time it takes you to leap over a garbage can on your skateboard. Plus, we are basically leaping from country to country. I swear, someday, I'm going to invent an amusement park ride called, "*The Leap*" and it's going to be the BEST RIDE EVER!

Here's what happens. We go in my closet and shut the door. Then, it feels like we're on a roller coaster in the dark. The closet disappears and turns the color of tie-dye, like my Uncle Matt's shirts. You always hear this loud rumble, which is just Hau's stomach and not really *Incidentally, Uncle Matt has long hair, which is SO RADICAL.* part of *The Leap*. Then, it feels like you shoot up a hill and drop down another. Your stomach falls down to your toes, and then you spin like you're inside of a s t r e t c h e d out Slinky. Then you're up and down, you shoot to the right, and then left and then swing upside-down . It's all over in about 2.5 seconds. It is SO FUN!

Landing is a different story.

As much as I love *The Leap*, I really hate the landings. We never know exactly where we are going to land, but we always land with a BANG, a BOOM, or a CRASH. We have never once landed on a stack of pillows or in a bounce house. Once, we landed in a big steaming pile of... well, I don't want to totally gross you out. Let's just say, I smelled like Hau for a while, but at least it was soft.

In Marrakech, Morocco, we landed with a THUD. That one hurt a bit. I lay on the ground looking at the sky, wondering for a second if maybe going to bed was better after all. Nah! On a pain scale from one to ten, it was only about a seven, which is better than going to bed. This ground was hard, but not like the sidewalk; more like really packed down dirt.

I sat up and looked around. We were at the top of a small hill. It looked like we were in the middle of nowhere. It was mostly flat, with little spiky bushes scattered around. In the distance I could see palm trees, but right around me was just this reddish brown dirt and rocks. Plus, it was hot. It was SO HOT!

Hau usually lands really close, sometimes even on top of me which is not fun. I landed on top of him once and almost squashed him flat. But, he just popped up and said, "I'm hungry." So, I knew he was fine.

This time, I couldn't see him anywhere. I stood up, shook the dirt off me and counted just two new bruises. Not bad.

"Hau, where are you man?" I called. I yelled a couple more times before I heard his muffled voice coming from inside one of the prickly bushes.

All I could see was his green foot sticking out of the bush. I really try to stay away from Hau's feet as much as possible, but I had no choice.

"Get me out of here!" Hau yelled.

To take my mind off his horribly stinky foot, I just pretended I was pulling a big chubby green carrot out of the ground. I went for it. I grabbed hold of his two-toed foot and yanked him clear out of the bush.

"Welcome to Marrakech, Morocco, Hau!" I held him upside–down as he dangled by one leg.

"Put me down or suffer the consequences!" He said. Man, he watches too much TV, I thought, as I set him down.

He counted his new bruises. "I got three", he told me. "You win, I just got two," I said. We always count. It's kind of a contest.

Hau danced around me in his very bizarre way and started singing, "I AM THE CHAMPION, MY FRIEND!" Seriously, this is one of those contests that I would rather lose.

What happened next always happens next. Hau was hungry.

"I'm hungry! I need some juice and some hangerbers and some soup and a chicken sand WITCH and some cookies and some..."

But, before he could even finish, a truck came speeding over the hill right toward us, kicking up a monster cloud of dust. It was an old blue pick-up truck with a trailer attached and it was not going to stop.

"WHOA, HAU LOOK OUT!!"

I grabbed Hau by his antennae and jumped out of the way, hitting the ground and rolling hard down a big hill.

I wasn't sure if we were ever going to stop rolling. I was tumbling and bumping and crashing, all while still holding onto Hau. Lucky for me, there was a fence at the bottom of the hill and it was nice enough to stop me. YOUCH! I realized then, that I had probably won the bruise contest after all.

I told you this was dangerous.

Hau finished his list. "...and a whole pie and a shake of milk."

Nothing can stop Hau when he's hungry.

The dust finally settled and I could see again. We had rolled right to the edge of an old farm. Then, we saw the kid and I knew we had arrived.

11

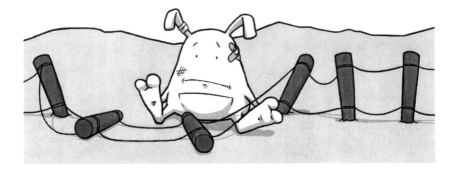

3 THE KID

I knew it was the right kid because it's always the first kid we see. Don't ask me how it happens, it just does.

I hopped up off the ground because it was getting SO HOT lying there.

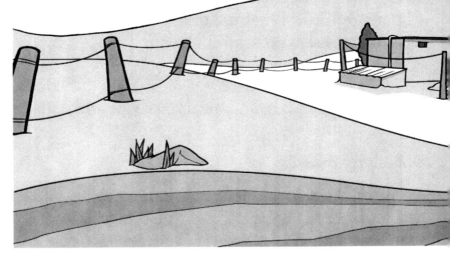

In the summer, my friend Badger (his real name is Jake) and I go to the beach and have contests to see who can stand on the burning-hot sand the longest. We pretend like we're standing on hot coals. I wonder who would have won in Marrakech? Probably me.

I think the ground was even too hot for Hau because he was flying and he hardly ever flies. Don't ask me how he does it. I have no clue. He doesn't have any wings or wear a jet pack or anything when he flies. It's just one of those things that are SO COOL.

I leaned on the fence and looked around the farm. Almost everything was the color of dirt, the houses, the buildings, the barns, the camels, the trees, and of course, the dirt. The houses were flat on top, not like my roof at home.

You could have a club house on these roofs and not even risk your life. That would be SO AWESOME. Hau plopped down on the top of the fence and asked, "Is it time for breakfast yet, man?" I was just about to call out to the kid when something happened that pretty much always happens.

CRASH! The fence broke. Hau always breaks stuff, but it's always an accident. At least it saved me from having to call the kid because that sure got his attention. He came running right over.

His name was Taymir; we knew that from the Tellus. His clothes were kind of bizarre. He wore this long shirt thingy. He told me later it was called a *djellaba*, and he wore pants underneath. If you don't believe me, see for yourself.

Djellaba - pronounced, ja-LA-ba

All the guys in Marrakech wore them. It isn't bizarre there at all. It is totally normal.

Incidentally, a long time ago I used to pull my socks way up to my knees then roll them down so they looked like big donuts around my ankles. I thought it looked cool. I wore them to school and Charles Elliot just pointed and laughed at me all day. I don't do that anymore. It is totally **NOT** normal.

So, Taymir got to the fence and said "Hi" to me just like this:

"*Labas, Bonjour*, Hello."

He told me later that he was checking to see what language I spoke. Taymir can speak Arabic, French, and English. That is SO COOL.

Then what happened next always happens next. There is no way around it.

1. Hau hides. This time, we were lucky because he was already under the broken fence. Perfect.

2. I say, "Hi" and "Sorry" for whatever we broke.
3. I tell the kid I'm here to help.
4. The kid is totally confused because how the heck did I know to come and help?
5. I explain about Hau because:

   a) If someone sees him too soon or they are not ready, they could run off never to be seen again. Although that's never happened, it is a possibility.

   b) It's not nice to surprise people with a watermelon- sized, flying, bizarrely shaped, eat everything in sight, mega-galactic alien. You need to give them some warning. It's only fair.

6. The kid totally gets it because kids totally get stuff that adults don't get.
7. The kid tells us the problem.
8. We get moving.
9. WAIT — first, we feed Hau. Then we get moving.

Taymir liked Hau right away. All kids do, and so do animals. Did I mention that? Animals LOVE Hau. They usually follow him around like he's their mom or something. Plus, Hau can understand animal language. It comes in handy A LOT.

Taymir's problem was that two of his camels had disappeared. I was glad to hear this because it didn't seem like it would be so hard to find a couple of camels. Man, was I wrong.

Taymir lives on this farm – he calls it a ranch, but I really don't see the difference – and his family takes people on tours into the Atlas Mountains. He said the Atlas Mountains are super cool, but super dangerous, so people shouldn't just go wandering around not knowing what they're doing, or they could get eaten by something. He said there are leopards, monkeys, vipers, and there used to be bears, but the Atlas bear is now extinct. Definitely, not cool about the extinct bear but the other animals are super cool.

Taymir's family **does** know what they're doing. They've been doing it for, like, fifty years. They take people into the Sahara Desert too, which is double dangerous. He said you could get stuck in a sandstorm and never be seen again. The Sahara Desert is bigger than the whole United States.

So, people come from all over the place to ride Taymir's camels into dangerous, awesome places, and no one ever even dies because his family is professional in

Incidentally, I did not see any certificates to prove this.

dangerous, awesome places.

That is SO AWESOME.

Taymir's dad and uncles were away on a tour so he was on his own to find the camels. Lucky for him, he had Hau and me to help.

Taymir took us into the barn. There were still lots of camels in there. It seemed like he had plenty; I was surprised he could even tell that two were gone. It turns out that his whole family survives because of the health and safety of all the camels. It's how they make their money to buy food and clothes and stuff.

The camels all crowded around Hau and started licking his face. Pretty soon he was coated in camel slobber, which was SO GROSS, but he never minds slobber.

In Morocco, they have the kind of camel with only one hump, called dromedaries. The Moroccans call them "*Jmel*". As my grampa would say, "Who'da thunk?" Anyway, I'm calling them camels because it's way easier than dromedaries. *Pronounced - drom-i-dar-ees*

"We are missing our two younger camels, Sarra and Jelel. I checked the gate to make sure they did not just wander off, but it was still closed," Taymir told me.

This was when I smelled a rat. "Smelling a rat" is when you think something is not quite right. If you

18

smelled a rat for real, I bet it would smell not quite right too.

Hau stayed in the barn to get slobbered on some more and to talk to the camels while Taymir and I walked over to the gate.

I opened it up and looked around. There were some tire marks on the ground that led right up the hill that I had rolled down earlier. Then I spotted a grungy, old, crumpled thing on the ground.

It was a photograph but it was torn in half. I showed it to Taymir and he said that it looked like a house from the medina in Marrakech.

"What the heck is a medina?" I asked.

"It is the oldest part of Marrakech. It is a very big

marketplace. It is about twenty miles north of here," said Taymir.

"I bet that's where your camels are," I said. "You got robbed, man."

"Why would someone take our camels?"

"Who knows? But let's get going. Hau and I almost got run over by the truck that made those tire tracks, so they can't be too far away. I'm going to take a wild guess that the tracks head toward the medina."

"You are correct, Seymour," Taymir said.

I was not surprised. "Let's go!"

"Hey, dudes!" Hau called out to us. "Some-ting smells malicious!"

Hau walked out of the barn dripping in camel goo.

"You mean 'delicious,'" I told him.

"Dat's what I said, man."

We all smelled it. It smelled SO GOOD.

"Smells like mint," I said to Taymir.

"My aunt and mother are cleaning up breakfast. I am sure they are making some more mint tea. We love mint tea in Morocco. It's malicious," Taymir said, giving a wink to Hau.

Hau turned to me and said, "See Sey? It IS malicious." He cracks me up.

We went in the barn to hide while Taymir went to get Hau some food.

Hau told me what the camels said. "The camels say they was sleeping when two guys came and took their friends away. They say one guy was tall, skinny, wrinkly, and had a furry lip, and one guy was smaller with a hat on. They say the guys were very ugly like snake-faces!"

"Did they really say the snake-face part, Hau?" I had to ask because you never know with Hau.

"Um, not really. But I bet they are just like Lex Luthor, mixed with the Green Goblin mixed with Dr. Doom. Right, Seymour?"

I agreed just as Taymir walked in with a tray full of yummy stuff. Mint tea with tons of sugar, bread, butter, honey, and jam. Hau went to town. He shoved the pot of mint tea in his pouch and the rest was all gone in about seventeen seconds. I knew enough to snatch a piece of bread before it disappeared. I had never seen bread like this before. It was flat and long, and all folded on top of itself. It was SO GOOD.

Taymir quickly fed the rest of the camels and did about one hundred other chores super-fast without even complaining. As he worked, I told him what we knew so far.

"So, we're looking for two men. One tall and wrinkly, with a mustache, and one short, with a hat.

And they are leading two camels around."

"Ha! You just described about every man in Morocco," Taymir said.

"Sheesh! Well, we have more than that. We know they are driving a blue pickup truck with a trailer, and we have this." I held up the ratty, old half-photograph.

Taymir nodded, and even though he looked worried, he seemed pretty hopeful to me.

He swung a leather bag full of supplies over his shoulder and said he was ready.

"Let's hit the road, Jack!" Hau said.

I snatched Hau and stuck him in my backpack before he could talk me out of it. That's where he stays while we are out in public. Hau hates it, but we don't want anyone seeing him and then running off, never to be heard from again.

It was extra blazing hot now! Hau complained from inside the backpack that he was melting. I almost wished I had on a djellaba because my jeans were super sweaty and Taymir looked way cooler.

We left the farm or the ranch or whatever you call it and headed north towards the medina.

4 MEZYAN MEANS GOOD

Taymir told me we were going to this gigantic marketplace called the Djemma El Fna. I was like, "The WHAT?" It was really hard to say, but after about fifty-seven times, I was saying it like a real Moroccan. It was like saying "Jam Ma Al Fnah" kind of fast.

How to say Djemma El Fna like a pro:
1. Say "Jam" like what you put on toast.
2. Say "MA"- like when you yell for your mom cause you don't feel like getting up.
3. Say "Al" like in Weird Al.
4. Say the "F" sound with "Nah" like when you don't want something.
5. Now put it all together "Jam Ma al fnah".

While we were walking, he told me tons of stuff about himself. He said he loves playing soccer, but he called it football like they do in England.

He also said that he doesn't go to school because they don't even have schools near him. I was like, "Dude, you are so lucky!" Then, he said his mom and grandma teach him at home and he has to do school at home every day. He said he doesn't have a TV at home and I was like, "Dude, you are so unlucky." But, he said he gets to watch movies at his cousin's house in the city and he thinks Indiana Jones is SO COOL. Instead of "SO COOL," he said *MEZYAN*, which means "good" in Arabic.

"Let me out, man! My brains are boiling!" Hau shouted from inside the backpack.

Poor guy. I stopped to let him out for a while, seeing as there was absolutely no one around. Hau flew out of the backpack like a rocket.

"Ahhhhhhh. Air!!" He did his bizarre dance for a minute and then dug a giant fan out of his pouch.

"Sorry, bud, no plugs around here," I told him.

He reached in his pouch again and held up a big, orange extension cord. He had a big, hopeful smile.

"Nope. That won't help," I said.

Hau shrugged and stuffed everything back in his pouch. Man, that pouch is bizarre. I've stopped trying to figure it out. Taymir just stood there with his mouth open. I told him to close it before he caught a bug.

Suddenly, Taymir shouted, "LOOK!"

In the distance, I could see a truck heading our way. I got ready to run, because you never know what's going to happen on these adventures. Taymir was running, but he was heading *towards* the truck. I grabbed poor Hau and zipped him back in the backpack. He was not happy.

The truck was being driven by Taymir's neighbor from the next ranch. The neighbors where Taymir lives are like fifteen miles away from each other. He was tall and thin with a wrinkly face and a mustache. I was immediately suspicious. Hmmmm, I thought, could this be the guy who stole the camels?

His name was Hamza, and he was not the guy who stole the camels. Taymir said he rides into the city all the time with Hamza to get supplies for their ranches.

I was psyched we didn't have to walk anymore. I watched the dirt go by from the backseat as Taymir told Hamza about the missing camels. They talked in languages that I did not understand. I thought it was French. Then, I thought it might be Arabic. I even heard a little English. I did hear the word Jmel, which I remembered meant camel, so I got that much. Moroccans can speak a lot of languages. That is SO MEZYAN!

It was a super bumpy ride. I had to keep making loud noises to cover up Hau's complaints from inside the backpack. I'm sure Hamza thought I was bizarre.

I could see the city ahead of us. Everything was still the color of dirt. The buildings were short compared to back home, no skyscrapers in Marrakech. There was one building that stuck up way higher than all the others.

"Get me out, mister!" Hau called in a muffled voice.

27

"Whoa! Check out that tower!" I yelled, louder then I needed to. Taymir heard Hau, too, and started talking loud to help me out. He pointed to the tower.

"It's the Koutoubia Mosque, a place where we go to pray; the largest mosque in Marrakech. It is very famous and beautiful. The tower is called a minaret; it is the oldest in the whole world. A legend says that those four balls on the top used to be made of solid gold!" Taymir shouted.

The road got super crowded with people as we approached the city. We decided to walk the rest of the way and hopped out. "Shoukran bazzef." Taymir said to Hamza and he put his hand on his heart. In case you didn't figure that out, it means, "Thank you very much." Obviously.

We were just a couple of blocks to the gate of the Djemma El Fna. I remembered how to say it that time.

In case you forgot, it's like, "Jam Ma Al Fnah", kind of fast.

As we walked, Taymir told me what Hamza said. Turns out, Hamza heard that two camels were just stolen from the Ahmed Ranch, too. He said they took two of the younger ones, just like Sarra and Jelel.

I knew I smelled a rat. Thieves. I unzipped the backpack a teensy bit to give Hau some air, and he forced the zipper open and leapt into the air. You won't even believe what happened next. This is worth a list.

1. Hau suddenly shrieked like this, "WAH HOOOO!"

2. Taymir and I nearly jumped out of our skin.

3. Hau started running as fast as his short legs and squashy body would take him (which is surprisingly fast) yelling... "I SMELL FOOOOOOOOOOOODDDDDD!"

4. Taymir and me chased after him yelling things like, "Stop!", "Wait up!", "You'll get lost!", and "Someone will see you!" Stuff like that.

Suddenly, Hau stopped in his tracks, and his jaw dropped down to the ground.

Now, I have to remind you that Hau has traveled throughout the universe, and has seen stuff that is SO AWESOME you can't even imagine it. I couldn't move either. I could only stare. We had arrived at the Djemma El Fna, and it was very, very, very *MEZYAN*.

5 AN EXPLOSION... OF COLOR

Whoa. I mean, WHOA! Really, what I meant was HOLY COW! This place is going to be hard to describe, so you will have to prepare all your senses to imagine this. The medina was ALIVE. It was like a carnival, or a circus... without the clowns. I was glad about that because clowns kind of freak me out. This was SO COMPLETELY, TOTALLY COOL! Lucky for you I got out my camera.

Let's start with SEEING:

I saw this HUMONGOUS open space filled with tons and tons of people. Like an outdoor mall.

I saw musicians playing Moroccan instruments. These guys were sitting in different circles all over the place playing lotars, which are like guitars with four strings, and banging on drums. Taymir told me

the drums were called tablahs and that the part they pound on was made of goatskin. Cool.

I saw these crazy cone-shaped piles of spices in dark reds, greens, and browns; barrels of olives; colorful rugs, bright clothes, earth-colored pots, leather belts and a lot of things that I had never even seen before.

I saw kids in costumes dancing, men wearing giant hats and selling mint tea, and women with colorful scarves wrapped around their heads.

Some of the people were dressed like me and some were dressed like Taymir. After seeing nothing but brown dirt and sand for so long, this place was like an explosion of color.

Now for the SMELLS:

I have to say that the smells were a mixture of delicious ("malicious," if you ask Hau), bizarre, and flat out gross. The first thing I did was grab Hau and stuck him in the backpack.

"Sorry, bud," I said. I felt really bad about it, but I couldn't risk Hau being seen. When he smells food he forgets that he is a round, green, squashy, slightly smelly, creature, and just goes for it. It does not go over to well... anywhere in the world.

There were vendors stirring big-giant steaming pots, which smelled like stew to me. Lots of smoke hung in the air from all the food-sellers, and the smells all mixed together. You'll have to trust me, the smells were out of control.

I could smell a fish fry kind of smell. Taymir said it was fried sardines, which are SUPER POPULAR in Morocco.

The smells were torturing Hau. I could hear him whining in the backpack. I asked Taymir to help me pick out a snack for Hau.

Taymir walked over to a vendor and came back with what he called a pastilla. He said it was a meat pie.

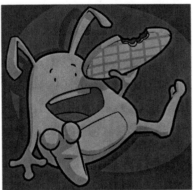

I stuck it in the backpack and I could feel from the bumping around that Hau was doing his bizarre dance. He was psyched!

We had to get moving. I pulled out the ripped photograph we found on the ground at Taymir's ranch. This was a big clue.

Taymir told me that the houses that looked like

the one in the photo were at the opposite end of the marketplace. Hopefully, we could find a match and find those camels!

We had a ways to walk, Taymir told me. After the outdoor market there were miles and miles and miles of covered hallways with more stalls and stores. Taymir said they were called 'souks' and they sell everything you could possibly want.

On a side note; Taymir was right about the description of the bandits. I saw lots of older men in Morocco that had mustaches and wore hats. Taymir says it's part fashion, part religion, part tradition.

Incidently, my Uncle Rick has a mustache. He's a policeman. A lot of his friends have mustaches too. Mustaches are popular in Morocco and in the police department. Isn't that bizarre?

6 PYRAMID OF DISASTER

We headed toward the large homes of the medina.

We walked by a bunch of men sitting cross-legged on colorful mats playing these little flutes. They reminded me of the recorders we had to learn in my music class. But, do you want to know the part that was SO COOL? They had these baskets in front of them, and after a few seconds, a snake would slither up out of the basket and dance around. SNAKES! SNAKES, I TELL YOU!! COBRAS! Did you know cobras are poisonous? Man, if my mom had given me a cobra, maybe I would have practiced the recorder more often.

I had to let Hau see this.

I took the backpack off my shoulder and set it on the ground. Hau wasn't squirming at all. I thought he was sleeping. I unzipped the bag and peeked in. I should have known better. Hau was crouched down like a frog.

"Hey, man!" Hau said, and in an instant, he sprang out of the backpack. He must have jumped ten feet in the air.

Luckily, everyone was too charmed by the snake charmers to notice. Hau landed like a wet sponge on the ground, and scooted under Taymir's djellaba. That long shirt does come in pretty handy.

Hau peeked out from under the djellaba and was amazed at the cobras, too. "Yikes! He gonna get his head bit off!" Hau said.

Although Hau has a way with animals, he is still afraid of snakes. He doesn't like spiders, either. And chihuahuas REALLY freak him out.

Although the snake charmers were SO AWESOME, we had to keep

moving because Sarra and Jelel were still missing.

Hau stayed under Taymir's djellaba. The marketplace was so loud and hectic, everyone looked too busy to notice Hau, anyway.

We walked through one section and there must have been a hundred carts all selling the same exact thing. Orange juice.

I was like, "Whoa, what's up with all these oranges?"

Taymir told me that they are the national fruit of Morocco, and there even used to be pictures of oranges on some of their money. Cool! We don't have any fruit on our money.

Each cart was pretty much the same. Big, old-fashioned looking wheels, a cloth roof above the counter, a clear-glass window where you could watch them squeeze juice, and piles and piles of oranges. Some were stacked neatly in a line, and some were built-up like a big pyramid of oranges.

The guys behind the carts were all yelling things in Arabic or French or German or English. It was loud and crazy and SO COOL! I figured they were yelling, "Come buy some oranges and freshly squeezed juice," because what else would they be yelling, really?

Just then, an orange juice vendor blocked our path and yelled really loud into my face, "Want some juice, young man?" He had this booming voice that reminded me of the principal at my school. Principals freak me out. This guy freaked me out, too.

How would you feel if some random guy shouted in your face?

I said "N-N-No, thanks."

"*La shukran*," said Taymir. I guess that means "No, thanks" in Arabic.

The orange juice guy ran off and tried to get two other people to buy some juice.

Just then, I saw something move out of the corner of my eye. It was Hau. He had come out from under Taymir's djellaba and was tiptoeing over to the oranges. That's when I thought "this is BAD NEWS."

Hau looked over his shoulder. Then he took an orange from the BOTTOM of the orange pyramid and was going to put it on the TOP.

"WAIT, Hau! NNNOOOOOOO!" I ran over to stop him, but it was too late. Hau smiled and plopped the orange on the top of the pile. He likes to do stuff like that, just to see what's going to happen.

I stood there in shock, waiting for the pyramid to rumble to the ground. None of the oranges fell. I was amazed.

"PHEW! You got lucky that time buddy. Now, knock it off!"

"O.K., no problemo," he said, but there was mischief in his eyes. Sometimes, I wonder if he'll ever get to go back to his planet.

Just as I was about to shove Hau into the backpack, I heard a familiar rumbling. UH OH! I covered my ears and hoped for the best.

Hau let out a ground-shaking BUUURRRPPP!

That was all it took. All of the oranges fell to the ground at my feet! Hau stuffed himself in the backpack and zipped it closed. So, there I stood. Five hundred oranges at my feet and no one else to blame. The orange juice guy stared at me.

"Whoops?" I said sheepishly.

Me and Taymir looked at each other and took off running. I could hear the orange juice guy yelling something at us. I'm assuming it wasn't nice. He chased after us at full speed.

I could hear Hau giggling as he bounced around in the backpack.

We were flying, weaving in and out of people and donkeys and guys carrying rugs on their heads. We turned a corner at super-duper speed and I "accidentally on purpose" tipped over a barrel of figs. It slowed down the orange juice guy, but kind of got the fig guy SO MAD. Once they untangled themselves we had:

1. Two super-mad guys chasing us
2. Tons of people and animals in our way
3. A backpack full of giggling alien
4. No camels

This was not good.

Just then Taymir said, "In here!"

We ducked under a large tapestry that was covering a doorway. I could hear my heart beating in my ears. It's SO WEIRD when that happens. Seconds later we saw two sets of feet run past yelling about figs and oranges. PHEW! We were safe.

Well. Not really.

7 THE SNAKE WHISPERER

"That was close," said Taymir.

"Really close," I agreed.

I opened my backpack and Hau popped out, smiling. I was about to give him a "what for?"

> Incidentally, my grampa is always talking about giving people a "what for." For example, I was driving with Grampa and this other car pulled out in front of us. We didn't get in an accident but Grampa said when we got up to the red light he was "gonna give that guy a what for." At the red light he started yelling at the guy but I never actually heard the words "what for," and he didn't "give" him anything. I just heard a lot of words that he told me I couldn't ever say in front of my mom.

Well, I was about to give Hau a "what for" when

I felt something move under my hand. It felt pretty big and a little cold. I grabbed it and held it up. I was about to ask Taymir what it was, when…

"AAAAAHHHH! That's a cobra!" Taymir shouted.

"AAAAAHHHH!" I shrieked.

"AAAAAHHHH!" Hau screamed. Poor Hau, he is useless when it comes to snakes.

Taymir whispered, "Don't move! Stay still. Cobras are deadly."

"No duh," I thought, everyone knows that. I don't think I could have moved if I tried.

I could see my reflection in the yellow eyes of the snake. I wasn't exactly sure how a cobra looks when it's about to strike and I really didn't want to find out. I realized quickly that I was glad my mom didn't buy me a snake to get me to practice my recorder.

Its tongue was flicking in and out of its mouth and its fangs were:

1. Really large
2. Really shiny
3. Really sharp looking
4. Really close to my face

Taymir began to chant a rhythm with words that

44

I didn't understand. It was like he was talking and singing at the same time. I have never stood that still in my entire life. Hau was frozen in place.

I don't know what Taymir did but the snake relaxed in my hand. It got really tired or something.

"Put the snake down very slowly. Very slowly, *beshwiya*," Taymir said softly.

Beshwiya = slowly (incase you didn't get that)

Once I put the snake on the ground, me and Hau carefully backed out from behind the rug. When we got back into the sunlight, I could barely stand. My legs felt like spaghetti and I fell into a heap on the ground. Hau stood there with his pouch pulled over his head. He does that sometimes, it's bizarre.

Taymir strolled out from behind a rug.

"You O.K., Seymour?" Taymir asked like it was nothing.

I was hot and cold at the same time and I wiped the sweat from my forehead.

"Yeah," was all I could say. Once I could speak, I asked Taymir how he did that.

"I know how to talk to snakes. My jeddah told me

45

it was my special gift. Jeddah means grandmother. She can talk to snakes, too," replied Taymir.

My grandmother has a special gift for knitting blankets, but I don't think that would have helped us in this situation. Now, if only I had a gift for finding camels.

8 THE CAMEL

Oranges, freaky cobras, food, mad dudes. Once again, we were finding more trouble than solutions. We did not have time for any more distractions.

Of course, you always get distractions when you have the least amount of time for them. My mom can vouch for this. I always distract her the most when she's super busy. I don't know why it happens. It's just the way it is.

Taymir started to get really worried. He led us through the narrow alleys and mazes of shops (or souks) and called loudly for Sarra and Jellel. Me and Hau were close behind. I scanned the streets in front of me while Hau peeked his eyes out of the backpack and looked behind us.

I took the ripped photograph out of my pocket

47

and looked at it again. It still didn't match anything around us. I even scanned it into the TELLUS but there just wasn't enough of the picture to pinpoint a location.

The sun was directly over our heads, which meant it was about noon. It was SO HOT outside, but the trail of Sarra and Jellel had turned very cold.

We started running, still looking carefully and still finding nothing but a few stray dogs and a handful of donkeys waiting to pull their carts back home.

Suddenly, Hau leaped out of my backpack and froze in mid-air in front of Taymir.

"Come on, Hau, we have to hurry. No more distractions!" I said.

Hau refused to move and lifted his nose to the sky.

"Hey, I smell something farm-mill-I-yer!" Hau said.

"NO MORE FOOD, DUDE!" I was exasperated. Mom says I'm exasperating sometimes, too.

Exasperated = Verb: irritate intensely; infuriate

"No food. No, no, no! LOOK! I smell camel!" Hau said.

Hau took us around a corner and down an alley where he pointed to a large, dusty area filled with donkeys, bikes, and motor scooters. There weren't too many people; just a few locking up their bikes to go off shopping.

Hau pointed to the far end of the lot. Sure enough, it was a camel. Hau had a good nose!

Now camels are not unusual in Marrakech but this one was not behaving usual. The camel was snorting and spitting and groaning loudly at some men that were leading her away. Taymir said camels don't act that way with their owners. As the camel jumped up to kick, we got a good look at the guys.

Tall Guy
  Thin √
  Wrinkly Skin √

Shorter Guy
  Hat √

Plus, it was super obvious that the camel did not belong to them. After a little fight, the camel finally let them lead it away.

"Is that one of your camels, Taymir?" I asked.

"No, it's not, but I think that there may be a connection."

I was thinking the same thing. This is what you call a "hunch." A "hunch" is when you have a feeling something might happen but you're not exactly sure. I had a HUGE HUNCH.

"Let's follow them!" I said.

Taymir looked hopeful and gave Hau a high-five as we carefully started to trail the bandits. Hau is SO AWESOME!

9 CAMEL BANDITS

Now we were getting somewhere! We were hot on their trail. As we followed the bandits, I noticed that there were fewer shops and more houses.

Go get a crayon and color this door blue!!

The houses didn't look like the ones where I live, at all. The doors were really big and were painted the color of the bluest ocean you can imagine. The houses were more like big buildings made out of hard clay. They were a reddish-

51

brown color, and all, kind of, smushed together, so it was hard to tell where one house ended and the next began. Bizarre. We had definitely entered a neighborhood.

I checked the TELLUS. We were heading west. Here's a hot tip for you:

It's always good to know what direction you're going, in case you need to get out fast.

We followed the bandits as close as possible, ducking and dodging behind whatever we could find when they turned around.

Want another hot tip?

Hiding behind a donkey is not a great idea for a lot of reasons.

Suddenly, the bandits stopped. They were at their destination. We were in front of a very familiar-looking home.

"I knew it! HA! Check this out guys." I pulled the

ripped photo out of my jeans, turned it just right and BLAM – a perfect match. The hunch was right, and so was my smelling of a rat!

"This is TOTALLY IT!" I said, a little too loud. Sorry, but sometimes I get excited. The bandits stopped just outside the door and began to walk our way. They heard me. RATS! We jumped into a cart full of hay and covered ourselves just in time.

"You're just being paranoid, boss," we heard the smaller bandit say.

> Paranoid is when you are freaked out about stuff you shouldn't be freaked out about. In my opinion, he had every reason to be paranoid. Seymour and Hau were coming for him!

They looked around for a bit and finally, after forever, the boss was satisfied. They opened the gate, dragged the poor camel inside, and closed it tightly behind them. We ran up to the gate just as we heard the click of the lock.

Now, we just had to get inside.

10 STRANGE NOISES

We could hear the bandits' muffled voices from behind the door.

"Let's split up," I said. "You guys go that way, check for any open windows or doors, I'll meet you around the other side."

Taymir and Hau found lots of windows, but the shutters were all locked up tight, and my side didn't have any windows at all.

After about 108 seconds, we all ended up at the back of the house. There we found a big, squarish window with a roundish top that had a fancy gate on it that we could see through. We were SO PSYCHED!

We crept up and peeked in and you will not believe what we saw.

A junk room. Yep- a room of junk. It reminded me of my garage back home.

Sometimes my mom makes me clean the garage, but I never actually get anywhere because there is way too much stuff to distract and amuse me in there.

Yes, this room was all junked-up like my garage, except for one thing. You know how most garages smell like gasoline? Well, this place had a smell that was more similar to:

1. The gorilla house at the zoo
2. The boys' locker room at school
3. My friend Tracey's backyard, she's got, like, ten dogs
4. HAU, when he eats too much fried food

It could only be #4. "Hau, dude, that's SO GROSS!" I said accusingly.

"That's not me this time, pal! You have the wrong man." Hau was offended.

"Yeah, right. I know that smell and it's definitely..."

Suddenly, Taymir clapped his hand over my mouth.

"SHHHHHHH – Listen, my camels!" Taymir said. His eyes... flying saucers.

The only thing you can do when your mouth is covered with someone else's hand is be quiet and listen... or bite them.

Strange noises were coming from somewhere. It sounded like muffled grunts and low groans, like a really, really long burp after you drink a full can of soda-pop real fast so your mom doesn't catch you.

We pressed our ears to the cracked-open window.

"How do you know that's coming from your camels?" I asked Taymir.

"I just know. Can you recognize the voices of your parents or friends when they call you?"

He had a point. I guess I'm just not used to camel voices.

"Well, it is no different. They can smell that I am

here and are calling to me. They have a very good sense of smell. They are scared! But, where is it coming from?" Taymir asked.

"They are under there!" Hau exclaimed with excitement.

"Under where?" I said.

"HA-- you said underwear! HA HA HA HA!" Hau burst into laughter. He loves getting me with that joke. I was about to finally give him that "what for" when it hit me.

Well, nothing actually hit me, I just figured it out, thanks to Hau's lame joke.

"Taymir, they are UNDER THE GROUND! There must be a trapdoor in there somewhere, and a room under the floor! That's why it's so hard to hear them and THAT'S WHY IT SMELLS IN HERE! Sorry for

blaming you, Hau."

"I accept your apology!" Hau said in a very professional way.

Taymir high-fived Hau again. Good old Hau. Hau smiled and danced around singing something about camels in underwear.

Camels, camels everywhere,

Over here and under there.

Under under underwear,

Camels, camels YAY!"

We had found Taymir's camels! Now, how were we going to get them out of there.

11 POUCH SUPPORT

A heavy, patterned rug was covering the floor of the junk room. I bet they bought that rug at the Djemma El Fna because it sure looked like the rugs we ran past earlier that day.

We needed some supplies. I asked Hau if he had anything that could move a rug. He smiled and pulled a wheelbarrow out of his pouch.

"Nice try, buddy," I said.

Then, I got a brilliant-beyond-brilliant idea.

Have I mentioned I have a knack for inventing stuff? This

invention was SO AWESOME, it deserves a list.

1. I grabbed three packs of watermelon gum out of my backpack. (What? I like gum!)
2. We all shoved five fat pieces of gum into our mouths.
3. I reminded Hau not to swallow his.
4. We drooled watermelon flavor.
5. Hau pulled a fifteen-foot pole out of his pouch. (sometimes he can read my mind)
6. I said, "SPIT!" and everyone spit their gum in to my hand.
7. I took all the soft, sticky gum and attached it to the end of the pole.
8. I slid the pole into a hole in the window where a small pane of glass was missing.
9. I dropped the sticky, gooey, gummy end of the pole on the rug.
10. I slowly lifted up the pole and the rug lifted.

We saw a trap door underneath!

It was quite the contraption. If you don't believe me, here are the blueprints.

It's just a preliminary sketch.

Preliminary, is when you have a first try real fast because you want to watch a show that's on in 2 minutes and 27 seconds, and you'll do a better job later.

Unfortunately, the list is not finished.

11. The gum got loose and the rug fell down with a loud FLOP.
12. We heard footsteps coming toward us.
13. The bandits heard us. Again.

Sheesh, do they have supersonic hearing or something?

12 THE AWFUL TRUTH

YIKES! I quick pulled out my brilliant invention and we ducked down just in time. We smashed ourselves really close to the house and held our breath, in case they peeked out the window.

The door opened and we heard both bandits come in the junk room.

"I know I heard something!" I remembered that voice from outside. It was the tall, old, wrinkly bandit. The boss.

"Why is the rug this way? I told you to keep it flat. *Mkellekh*!" he yelled.

"*Mkellekh*?" I mouthed the word to Taymir. He understood.

"It means 'stupid'," he mouthed back.

Oooo. How rude of him.

Incidentally, when you mouth words, you say them but no sound comes out. Try it.

The other bandit, the guy with the hat, argued back at the boss.

"I know I put it back the last time I fed them!! Do you smell dellah?" said the short bandit.

I was about to mouth, '*dellah*?' to Taymir when the boss answered my question for me.

"HOW CAN I SMELL WATERMELON, YOU DUNCE!?! All I can smell are those mangy camels!"

Ah. Got it. *Dellah = watermelon*. I guess the short bandit's nose was pretty good if he could smell our gum over the smell of the funky camels.

The boss continued to yell and that's when we found out the awful truth.

"The tour company will take all ten of them tonight! Our pockets will be full of dirham and we will be rid of those filthy, drooling beasts! Now FIX the carpet! We've got work to do! And shut the window!" yelled the tall bandit.

"All right, all right," said the short bandit and made his way toward the window, mumbling something about watermelon. We could hear the boss still yelling as they walked down the hall.

Taymir looked upset, scared, and angry all at the same time. He was SO FREAKED OUT!

"They are selling my camels to another tour company, TONIGHT! Those evil men! We have to get in!"

Lucky for us, I had a plan.

13 THE (1/4) PLAN

So, I know I said I had a plan before, but I actually had maybe only ¼ of a plan. I figured the other ¾

would come to me on the fly.

We needed to get in and there was only one way to do that. Go up. You see, in Morocco, they have these big courtyards in all their houses. I saw a bunch of them as we ran through the medina. It's like a big room with no ceiling. If you can get to the top of the wall, you just hop right in the courtyard and you're in. Simple. Then we grab the camels and get out.

65

We ran back to the side of the house. Hau flew up to the top of the wall to survey the situation.

He dropped back down to report.

"No gad buys," said Hau.

I was pretty sure he meant "bad guys."

"Excellent! Can you fly us up?" I asked.

"I'll try," Hau said.

Hau grabbed the back of my shirt with one hand and Taymir's djellaba with the other. Then he stopped.

"I'm hungry! I need a heart-healthy snack."

Have I mentioned that Hau loves to watch commercials?

Taymir had a loaf of bread in his leather supply bag. He handed it to Hau. Hau broke it in half, swallowed one half, and dropped the other half in his pouch.

"Fur later?" Hau smiled. Taymir stared at him. It really is amazing to watch Hau eat.

He held us tight again and began flying up the side of the wall, with us dangling like dolls from his hands. Luckily, the only onlooker was a very confused donkey.

We had almost reached the top when Hau began

to struggle. He's not the best flyer to begin with, even without the extra weight of two kids. I was beginning to have doubts about my ¼ of a plan.

I could tell Hau was exhausted and I felt really helpless as we bumped and smashed against the wall. I knew he wouldn't drop us because you never drop your friends. That's all there is to it.

Finally, Hau reached the top and we swung our legs over the wall. I grabbed a juice box out of my backpack and tossed it to Hau. He caught it in his mouth, smiled gratefully, and collapsed in my lap.

So there we were, balanced on top of the wall.

There was a huge tree hanging right above us. It was full of ripe, sticky, dates.

Incidentally: I know about dates because my grampa eats them all the time. They are a super-sweet fruit. He told me they would put hair on my chest if I ate them. Once I ate twenty-seven of them in a row and not one single hair grew on my chest. His theory is shot if you ask me.

Perched like birds on the wall, we could see the entire courtyard. It was SO COOL inside! It had a fountain in the center and a few trees growing in just the right spots. There were couches covered with dark purple and blue pillows and big pots full of plants with red flowers.

Taymir was confused.

"Why would such rich men steal camels from us? I do not understand," he wondered.

I had a hunch that they did not own this place. So far, my hunches have been 100% correct and I'll just tell you now, I was right. Again.

I grabbed my binoculars out of my backpack to check out the area. There were hallways leading in every direction off the courtyard. Nice and confusing.

"Taymir, over there." I pointed over to a hallway at the far corner of the courtyard. "I think that's the way to the camels."

"I think you are right. May I use those?" I handed Taymir my binoculars and he aimed them at a large family portrait on the far wall. This is when we started getting some answers.

Incidentally, my mom is always looking for "some answers" from me.

"HEY-- those are the people that went on a tour with my family this week!" he exclaimed.

"What?" Now, I was confused.

"The bandits must be the caretakers of the house! They knew the owners would be gone AND they knew all the men in my house would be away on tour. They thought it would be easy to steal the camels, hide them, and sell them off." Taymir was SO MAD!

"The people who live here will be back tonight. We have to hurry – the bandits will have to get the camels out of here soon. You were right, Seymour. Those rats!"

Taymir continued to put the pieces together.

"And they knew my camels would go easily because they are so gentle and used to different people." He got even angrier as he spoke, "We must stop them NOW!"

"SHHHHH! Bad guys," said Hau.

We hid in the branches of the date tree just as the camel bandits walked into the courtyard.

14 THE (1/2) PLAN

The two bandits strolled into the courtyard and laid down on long, cushioned chairs directly below where we sat. I thought they said they had a lot of work to do, but they didn't seem very busy. It seemed bizarre to me.

Bizarre, but perfect. More of my plan came to me just then. I had about ½ a plan now! We would walk along the wall and Hau would fly us down near the hallway where the camels were. If we were quiet, they would never hear us.

The shorter bandit was looking at a photo album full of images of the family that lived in the house. "Are you still looking at those photos? Put that down and get me some tea," the boss ordered.

"All those camels look young and strong. I think

the tour company will see that and we'll get a hefty price," the boss yelled. He was a loud talker!

They seemed pretty distracted to me. It was time to make our move. I did one of those 'pssst' noises and motioned for Taymir and Hau to follow me. We carefully stood up and balanced on the high wall. We started walking toward the hall where the camels were being held. It felt like a circus act. The death-defying tightrope walkers!

Taymir was behind me while Hau quietly hovered after him.

It was a slow and scary walk.

"Don't look down," I whispered. I was sort of reminding myself most of all. Heights are not my favorite thing.

We had not gotten very far, when a strong gust of wind caught Hau unexpectedly and pushed him into Taymir's back. Taymir stumbled and let out a tiny yelp. Hau quickly grabbed Taymir and steadied him back up on the wall. It wasn't a very loud yelp... but it was loud enough. This was SO NOT *MEZYAN*!

The short bandit saw us first.

"HEY, BOSS! LOOK!" he yelled, pointing up.

"Change of plans!" I shouted. "Bombs away!"

I grabbed some dates off the tree and started whipping them down at the bandits. They may not grow hair on your chest but they sure do splat nicely when thrown upon heads and faces.

Taymir looked down and saw a tapestry hanging on the wall right below us. He reached down, grabbed it, and quickly swung down along the wall. That was SO SWEET!

Tapestry = A big cloth that hangs on the wall, kind of like a painting that is made out of material.

The moment Taymir's feet hit the hard tile floor, he ran to the hallway we hoped would lead us to the camels. Taymir was SO FAST! I'd hate to race him on the playground!

The short bandit was right on Taymir's heels. Hau came to the rescue! He flew off the wall, stopping just above the bandit's head.

Then he:

1. Reached into his pouch
2. Pulled out the pot of mint tea he had gotten at Taymir's house
3. Dumped it directly on the bandit's head

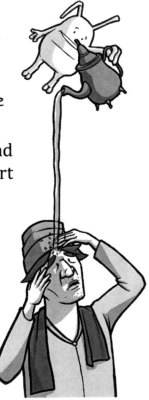

"YAAAAAAAAAAAAAA! My head is on fire!" screamed the short bandit.

"OOOOOOO-- still hot!" said Hau. He poured the rest of the tea into his mouth and dropped the empty pot on the bandit's head, knocking him down.

"What the..?" cried the

bandit, holding his head.

Taymir raced toward the hallway but was cut off by the boss. He quickly spun around and disappeared down another hallway. This place really was like a maze! The boss followed.

I grabbed on tight to a branch from the date tree, held my breath, and jumped. I was hoping the branch would gently lower me to the floor. Not quite. I landed directly on my rear-end. Not fun.

The short bandit had recovered and was standing right over me, smirking. Smirking is like smiling when you're evil. Somehow, he looked taller from this angle.

"Got you now, you little punk!" he shouted.

"Who are you callin' 'punk'?" I asked.

You see, I still had the branch in my hand, so I was not the one in trouble here. I let go of it and WHAP! It sprang back with some serious force, smacking the

bandit in the face and launching him backwards into the fountain. SO AWESOME!

"Looks like you're all wet, dude! Hau, keep him busy!" I yelled, and took off running for Taymir.

Hau lounged in one of the cushioned chairs, munching on the rest of the loaf of bread. He pulled random items out of his pouch and threw them at the very frustrated bandit every time he tried to get out of the fountain. A moldy sandwich, a broken doorknob, empty shampoo bottle... kinda like spring-cleaning for the pouch.

There were way more hallways and doors in the house than I expected, and I got totally lost. I heard running footsteps so I jumped into this huge basket nearby. Through the holes in the woven basket I saw Taymir run past.

"Taymir, over here," I hissed.

Taymir stopped and hopped into a matching basket next to mine.

We hid silently – barely breathing – while we waited for the boss to pass.

Seven seconds later, the boss ran by, yelling for his partner.

"WHERE ARE YOU, YOU USELESS WRETCH? WE'VE GOT TO GET THESE *DRERRI*!"

Incidentally, 'drerri' means kids, and he was not gonna get THESE drerri!

Phew! That was close! We waited for the footsteps to disappear, leaped out of the baskets and dashed down the hall.

15 THE (3/4) PLAN

"It's this way!" said Taymir. "I can hear them."

I followed Taymir to the junk room. The door was locked! Like that was going to stop us. We both stepped back and without even saying anything, we rammed our shoulders into the door. Sometimes, words are not necessary.

It didn't budge, so we stepped back and went for it again. This time it flew open and launched us into the room. We both landed in a heap on top of the trapdoor. Bruise #8.

"That was SO COOL!" said Taymir. I think I was starting to rub off on him.

We whipped back the rug and opened the trapdoor underneath it.

A wide ramp led to an underground room filled with ten camels. The camels started growling and roaring. It sounded like a room full of sea lions mixed with the world's biggest burping contest.

"SARRA! JELEL!" Taymir rushed down the ramp to hug his camels. They nuzzled his face and got all kinds of camel slobber all over him. Taymir was so happy to see them, he didn't seem to mind.

The other camels were scared but Taymir quickly calmed them with his voice. He walked to each camel, said something in Arabic, and gently petted each one, from forehead to nose.

"Take the ropes and help me lead them out of here. They will all follow once we begin," said Taymir.

I grabbed the ropes for Jelel (at least I think it was Jelel), and started toward the ramp, but it was too late. Both bandits were standing at the exit with large sacks.

The boss looked SO MAD! Sometimes my mom says she is 'positively furious' with me. I believe this guy had that same sort of look.

The short bandit was soaking wet, covered with sticky date goo, and looked very irritated. They threw a sack over each us and dragged us up the ramp.

We heard the camels spit and charge at them, but they were lashed back by a whip from the boss.

Once the bags were over our heads, the bandits roughly tied us up and shoved us into a corner.

"What business do you have with my camels?!?" barked the boss bandit. Yikes— he was a really loud talker!

"Those camels do not belong to you! You will pay for this!" yelled Taymir from inside his sack.

"More like, I will get paid for this!"

snickered the evil boss. "Come on, the buyers will come soon. We must lead the camels out of here."

I have to admit, I had a hunch we were in trouble.

16 THE (WHOLE) PLAN

We could hear the bandits leading the camels into the courtyard as we struggled to get out of the sacks.

I knew Hau would be lost in the labyrinth of hallways. "HAU – NOW!" I shouted. It took 4.2 seconds for him to show up. It's our emergency call.

Hau poked his head in the underground room. "Where have you been all my life?" he asked.

Hau quickly untied the ropes and ripped off the sacks. We were on our feet in an instant and racing to the courtyard.

Taymir called to his camels, making a low bass drum sound with his voice.

Immediately, Sarra and Jelel pulled away from the bandits and ran to Taymir. All of the other camels

began to pull away, too.

Soon, the bandits could not hold on anymore.

They tried to control the camels but they had no luck. The camels were now running around the courtyard like… well, like animals. The bad guys had been beaten!

The bandits opened the big blue doors to escape, but too bad for them! As soon as the camels noticed the open doors, they stampeded through them to get out. They knocked down those dirty rats and took off into the streets toward their homes.

The bandits lay on the ground, coughing from the dust and aching from the hoof prints on their backs.

The only camels that remained were Sarra and Jelel and one pokey camel who proudly clomped across the bandits' backs and even paused to "go potty" right above them, before he plodded down the alley.

Hau walked over to the bandits and took a big whiff.

"EWWWWWWW, you stink!" Hau said, as he held his nose. He reached in his pouch and squirted them with bubbly soap.

Me and Taymir were laughing so hard, we could barely climb on the camels' backs.

The bandits growled and tried to get up but fell, exhausted, to the ground.

Taymir and I rode Sarra and Jelel out of the courtyard with Hau hanging on tightly to Sarra's tail. This was my plan all along. Simple.

The owners of the home were standing speechless at the blue doors. They stared at their beautiful courtyard (now a disaster) and at the bandits on the ground and at me and Taymir.

Hau hid behind the camels.

Taymir quickly explained what happened. He spoke in Arabic again so all I got was "Jmel," but they looked pretty angry. The father shook his fist at the battered bandits and flipped open his cell phone. The cops were on their way and so were we.

We steered the camels down the street and toward home.

17 BACK AT THE RANCH

The sights, sounds, and smells of the Djemma El Fna began to fade as we rode south, back toward Taymir's place.

Taymir said the marketplace is even busier at night, with more snake charmers, story-tellers, fortune-tellers, dancing monkeys, and tons more food. (He said the food part really softly, which made me think he was getting the hang of Hau.) He said it's like a huge party at the marketplace EVERY NIGHT! I could tell he was proud of his country.

"That is SO SWEET! Maybe I can show you around *my* town someday," I said.

I really meant it, too. I wasn't just saying that to be polite like my mom makes me do with my out-of-town cousins. I would LOVE to introduce Taymir to my buddy, Badger. Maybe Taymir can use his animal skills to actually calm a real badger long enough so we can pet it. Plus, my mom would like him too, he has way better manners then me, I think.

We got to Taymir's ranch just as the sun was setting in the African sky. The gold of the sun had changed to orange. It reminded me of the oranges at the medina. It had been a seriously crazy, highly dangerous, incredibly interesting day, and I know one thing for sure; Marrakech, Morocco is SO AWESOME!!

Taymir's family ran out to meet us. I grabbed Hau and zipped him in the backpack. I knew there was food nearby and I was not ready for another adventure just yet.

Taymir told his family the whole story. They called me *Al-batal*. Which means "hero" in Arabic. If only

my mom knew how helpful I am!

They even invited me to have dinner on the ranch.

"Thanks, but I have to get home!" I said.

"AWW, MAN – DINNER!" wailed Hau from in the backpack. I had to hold the zipper so he wouldn't get out, and I had to yell out random things like, "LOVELY TO MEET YOU," "I'M OFF TO THE RACES," and "TAYKIDEEZY!"

Taymir walked us to the edge of the ranch, where we had all first met. He thanked us again and again and said that if we ever needed anything, to give him a call. "You will always have a friend in Marrakech," Taymir said, as he stuck out his hand.

"And you will always have a *saheb* in New York," I said, remembering Taymir's word for friend.

We shook hands. Just then Hau popped out of the backpack and threw his arms around Taymir for a big, squashy, slightly slimy hug.

"You're my friend, too?" Hau smiled hopefully.

"Yes, Hau. I'm your friend, too. I will forever be grateful!

"*Shukran*," said Taymir.

"See you around, man!" I said.

"See you around, man!" Said Hau. He likes to copy.

Taymir stood and waved as we walked away. Hau pulled out the Tellus and pushed the "LEAP HOME" button.

The leap home is exactly the same as the leap that takes us all around the world EXCEPT... backwards.

Like this:

1. You swing upside-down
2. Shoot left
3. Shoot right
4. Go down, then up (like a wave)
5. Slinky Spin
6. Stomach falls down to your toes
7. Drop down a hill
8. Fly Up a Hill
9. Hear a loud RUMBLE (that's really Hau's stomach)
10. Step out of the closet and into my bedroom.

It is SO FUN! You HAVE to try it sometime.

18 HOME

We always get back at the same exact time we left, which is bizarre when you're traveling halfway across the whole world. Don't ask me how it works, it just does.

Whenever I go to the store with my grampa he ALWAYS says, "Back the same day we left." I never really get that because obviously we're getting back the same day we left; the store is only three blocks away.

I lay in my bed, flipping through *The Guinness Book of World Records*, I was looking for the world's most deadly snakes and the world's hottest climate, because I was pretty sure I experienced both in Marrakech. Oddly, cobras are not even in the top ten of deadliest snakes. But, the Sahara Desert IS one of the hottest places on earth.

I could hear Hau snoring away in the closet.

"Meat, camels, rice, snakes, food, oranges, mint tea..." mumbled Hau. He always talks in his sleep.

I have this huge world map in my room. My mom almost passed out when I asked for it. She's not used to me asking for anything but video games, but I think maps are SO COOL!

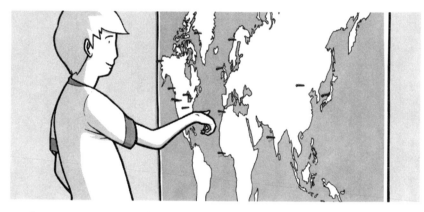

I sat up on my bed and found Africa on my map. I pushed a thumbtack way up in the northwest corner, into Marrakech, Morocco. It's my personal tradition.

You know how I told you that I hate going to bed? Well, I decided to close my eyes for a quick rest, and I fell asleep in 12.4 seconds. Isn't that bizarre?

M'a ssalama! Good Bye!

THE END

Melanie Morse and Thomas McDade currently live Buffalo, NY where it's actually pretty great. You should all come and check it out. When they aren't walking their super cute dog, Honey, or traveling with some particularly fun kids (also quite cute) they can be found producing and directing video projects and commercials with their company Honey + Punch.

seymourandhau.com

CPSIA information can be obtained at www.ICGtesting.com
Printed in the USA
BVOW04s2019111114

374664BV00001B/3/P

9 780692 298343